*Aladdin* and *Ali Baba* are two tales from
*The Arabian Nights*, a collection of
stories dating back at least to the fifteenth century.
No one knows for certain where the stories
originated – scholars think it may have been
Persia or Egypt. The narrator of the tales
is the beautiful Scheherezade, who is supposed
to have told her husband, King Shahriyar,
a new story every night for 1,001 nights, to keep him
from killing her. That is why the stories
are also called *The Thousand and One Nights*.

*Acknowledgment*
Line illustrations by John Lawrence

**Ladybird**

Ladybird books are widely available, but in case of
difficulty may be ordered by post or telephone from:

Ladybird Books – Cash Sales Department
Littlegate Road  Paignton  Devon TQ3 3BE
Telephone 01803 554761

A catalogue record for this book is available
from the British Library

Published by Ladybird Books Ltd  Loughborough  Leicestershire  UK
Ladybird Books Inc  Auburn  Maine 04210  USA

© LADYBIRD BOOKS LTD 1995
LADYBIRD and the device of a Ladybird are trademarks of Ladybird Books Ltd

*CLASSIC FABLES
AND LEGENDS*

# ALADDIN

# ALI BABA

*Retold by Molly Perham
Illustrated by Francesca Pelizzoli*

*A stranger stood watching Aladdin*

In a large city in China there once lived a tailor called Mustapha. He was very poor, and found it hard to provide enough food for himself, his wife and his son, Aladdin.

When Aladdin was old enough to learn a trade, Mustapha began to teach him how to use a needle. But Aladdin was lazy, and preferred to play in the streets with his friends. There was nothing Mustapha could do to make Aladdin work. The poor tailor became ill with worry, and soon he died.

Aladdin's mother thought that surely now Aladdin would earn some money. But time went by, and Aladdin was just as lazy as ever. They had to manage with only the money the widow earned herself by spinning cotton.

One day a stranger stood watching Aladdin as

he played in the street. The stranger was a magician, and thought that Aladdin appeared to be just the kind of boy he was seeking to carry out his plan.

'Is Mustapha the tailor your father?' called the magician to Aladdin.

'He was,' said Aladdin. 'But he is dead.'

The magician threw his arms round Aladdin and kissed him. Tears rolled down his cheeks.

'I have come too late,' he sobbed. 'Your father was my brother. I have been all over the world trying to find him.'

Then the magician asked Aladdin where he lived, and gave him some money. 'Take this to your mother and tell her that I will come and see her tomorrow.'

Aladdin ran home immediately. 'Mother!' he called. 'My uncle came up to me in the street today and gave me this money to help us. He wants to come to visit us tomorrow.'

'Uncle? You have no uncle,' said Aladdin's mother. She did not know what to think. Her husband had never spoken of a brother. But they were poor and hungry, so she kept the money and used it to buy food for their supper.

The stranger came as promised, and said that he would like to set his nephew up in a shop, so that he could make a good living. To prepare him, he took Aladdin into the wealthy parts of the city and bought him fine new clothes.

Then one day they set off through the city gates, past large palaces with lovely gardens, until at last they came to a narrow valley between two mountains.

'Now you will see wonderful things that no one has ever seen before,' said the magician. 'Gather some dry sticks to kindle a fire.'

When the fire was blazing fiercely, he threw incense into the flames and spoke some magic words. The ground shook beneath their feet and opened up to reveal a square stone with a brass ring in the centre.

Aladdin was so frightened that he wanted to run away, but the magician caught hold of him. 'You have seen my power,' he said firmly, 'and now I want you to do something for me. Pull that stone up by the ring.'

Aladdin took hold of the ring, and found he could lift the stone with hardly any effort. Below the stone there was a cave with steps leading down into darkness.

'Listen carefully,' said the magician. 'Go down into that cave, and at the bottom you will find a door that leads into three great halls. In each hall you will see four large brass vessels full of gold and silver. Do not touch them, and take care that you do not touch the walls, or you will die instantly. At the end of the third hall there is a door that leads into a garden of fruit trees. Walk straight along the path, although you may pick

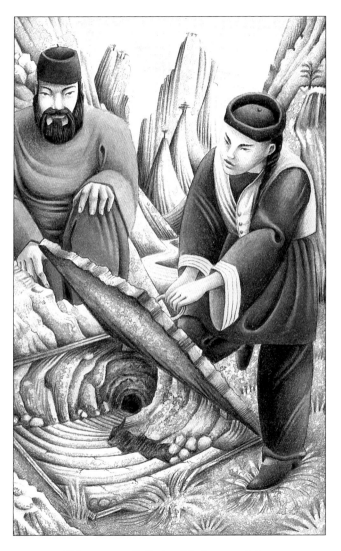

*'Listen carefully,'* said the magician

some of the fruit along the way if you wish. At the end of the path you will find a lamp in a niche of the wall. Bring the lamp to me.' After he had given these instructions the magician took a ring off his finger.

'This ring will keep you from harm,' he told Aladdin. 'Now do as I say, and we will both be rich for the rest of our lives.'

So Aladdin went down into the cave and found the three halls and the garden, just as the magician had described them. The trees were loaded with extraordinary fruit of many different colours. Some were pure white, and others as clear as crystal; some were pale red, and others green, blue, purple and yellow. He could hardly believe the dazzling sight before him.

Aladdin took down the lamp and tucked it into his waistcoat. Then he filled his pockets with fruit and returned through the three halls and up the steps, where the magician waited for him.

'Give me the lamp,' said the magician harshly, 'and you will be able to get out more easily.'

'No,' said Aladdin, who was beginning to distrust the man who claimed to be his uncle. 'Help me out first, and then I will give you the lamp.'

Neither of them would give way to the other. The magician became enraged and, shouting some magic words, threw more incense into the fire. The stone fell back into place, trapping Aladdin inside the cave.

For two whole days Aladdin remained helpless in the cave. On the third day, when he had given up hope of ever seeing daylight again, Aladdin put his hands together to pray. As he did

*'I am the slave of the ring'*

so, he happened to rub the ring that the magician had given him. At once an enormous genie appeared before him.

'I am the slave of the ring,' said the genie. 'What is your wish?'

'Get me out of this place,' said Aladdin.

The earth opened, and Aladdin found himself back where the fire had been. With great relief, he ran home to tell his mother all about the cave and the lamp, and to give her the fruit.

Next morning there was no bread in the house for breakfast.

'I will sell some of the cotton I have spun,' said Aladdin's mother, 'and then I can buy food.'

'No, keep your cotton, Mother,' said Aladdin. 'I will sell the lamp from the cave instead.'

'It will fetch a better price if I clean it,' the widow said, and she began to polish and rub the lamp. At once a genie stood towering before her.

'I am the slave of the lamp,' he roared in a

voice as loud as thunder. 'Tell me your wish and I will grant it.'

The widow was so frightened she could not speak. But Aladdin took the lamp and said, 'We are hungry. Bring us something to eat.'

The genie disappeared. A moment later he was back, with all sorts of good things on gold and silver plates.

Aladdin's mother stared in amazement. 'Where can all this have come from?' she asked.

'The lamp must be magic,' said Aladdin.

'Then take it away quickly,' said his mother. 'I want nothing to do with evil spirits.'

After that, whenever they needed food, they sold one of the plates. Aladdin also bought fine clothes, and became quite a gentleman.

Some years later Aladdin, now a man of some wealth and fortune, was walking in the town. He happened to see Princess Badroulboudour, the sultan's daughter, riding on horseback. Aladdin could hardly believe how beautiful she was. He fell in love with her instantly.

That night Aladdin told his mother that he wanted to marry the princess. He knew that the sultan would often allow his people to come to him and ask favours. Aladdin begged his mother to go to the palace and speak to the sultan on his behalf.

His mother told him not to be so foolish. 'What chance have you of marrying a sultan's daughter?' she said. 'Have you forgotten how humble our background is?'

Aladdin thought for a moment and then remembered the fruits he had brought from the cave. He realised now that they were precious stones of great value. He fetched the jewels and laid them out on the table. They shone so brightly that mother and son were nearly blinded by their brilliance.

'Take these to the sultan,' said Aladdin, 'and I am sure he will give you whatever you ask for.'

So Aladdin's mother wrapped the jewels in a fine cloth and set off for the palace. There was a large crowd of people at court waiting to speak to the sultan. Although she stood at the front, Aladdin's mother was not one of those chosen. Disappointed, she returned home.

Next day Aladdin's mother returned to the palace, and the same thing happened. This went on for several days, until at last the sultan took pity on her and asked what she wanted.

The widow told the sultan how her son had fallen in love with Princess Badroulboudour and wished to marry her. She untied her bundle and gave him the jewels. 'These are a present for Your Highness, from my son,' she said.

*'These are a present… from my son'*

The sultan had never before seen such wonderful jewels. He turned to his vizier and said admiringly, 'Whoever sends such a present must surely be worthy of my daughter's hand in marriage.'

Some time before this, the sultan had told the vizier, who was his most important minister, that the princess would marry his son. Now the vizier was afraid that this promise might be forgotten. Worried, he whispered something softly in the sultan's ear.

The sultan nodded gravely and turned to Aladdin's mother. 'Go home and tell your son that I cannot give my daughter to him for three months. Return here at the end of that time.'

Three months later, Aladdin's mother went back to court.

'Sir,' she said, 'I have come to remind you of your promise to my son. Three months have gone by. What may I tell him?'

When the sultan turned the widow away, he had thought that she would never come back. He asked his vizier what he should do next.

'Set such a high price on your daughter that he will not be able to pay it,' suggested the vizier.

So the sultan said to Aladdin's mother, 'Tell your son I will keep my word as soon as he sends me forty large basins made of the purest gold, filled with precious stones like those you have already given me, and carried by forty slaves.'

Aladdin was waiting eagerly to hear his mother's news. When she told him what the sultan had said, she added, 'I think it best that you forget the princess, my son. I do not suppose for a moment that you will be able to meet the sultan's demands.'

But as soon as she had gone out, Aladdin took the lamp and rubbed it. The genie appeared at once and asked him again: 'What is your wish?'

21

*People stopped to watch… the exotic procession*

Aladdin told the genie what he wanted. In a very short time the genie came back, bringing with him forty slaves dressed in silk robes that were decorated with many precious stones. Each slave carried a gold basin full of jewels.

'Go to the court with these at once,' said Aladdin to his mother. 'Tell the sultan they are for him.'

People stopped to watch as the exotic procession wound its way through the streets to the palace. They had never seen such riches before. The sultan, too, could hardly believe his eyes. At last he turned to the vizier and said, 'Well, vizier, what do you say now?'

It was the vizier's duty to make a reply that would please the sultan, so he said, 'Sir, the greatest treasure in the world should not be compared to Princess Badroulboudour.'

But the sultan no longer hesitated. The sight of such immense riches persuaded him that

whoever had sent them was worthy of his
daughter. 'Go, my good woman,' he said
to Aladdin's mother, 'and tell your son that
I welcome him with open arms.'

The widow lost no time in telling her son what
had happened. Aladdin went to his room and
fetched the lamp. No sooner had he rubbed it
than the genie appeared to do his bidding again.

'Genie,' said Aladdin, 'I want the most
magnificent robe that anyone has ever seen, and
a horse more splendid than any in the sultan's
stable. The saddle, bridle and harness should be
made of the finest leather, studded with jewels.
Then bring me twenty richly dressed slaves to
walk by my side, and twenty more to walk in
front. I also want ten thousand pieces of gold in
ten purses.'

When the genie had brought everything he
asked for, Aladdin mounted the horse and set off
for the palace. The streets were thronged with

people, who shouted and cheered as the slaves threw the gold pieces among them.

The sultan was delighted to see that Aladdin was young and handsome as well as rich, and the princess fell in love with him at first sight. The sultan gave orders for the marriage to take place right away.

'Before I marry the princess, I must prepare a home for her,' said Aladdin. So that night he rubbed the lamp again and said to the genie, 'Build me a house of the finest marble set with precious stones. The furniture shall be of solid gold, and the gardens full of the sweetest-scented flowers.'

Next morning the house was ready. Aladdin married the princess, and for some time they lived in happiness.

All this time, the magician had been away from China. It was not long before he heard that Aladdin had not only become a rich man, but also a prince, and that his princess was the lovely Badroulboudour, daughter of the sultan. He knew that Aladdin must still have the lamp, and he thought of a clever plan to get it back from him.

The magician bought some new lamps, and waited until Aladdin had gone away for a few days. Then he walked up and down the streets outside the house calling out, 'New lamps for old! New lamps for old!'

Princess Badroulboudour heard him calling and thought of the old lamp that Aladdin kept beside his bed. She did not know why he bothered to keep it. 'How pleased he will be to have a new one,' she said to her maid, and she sent the girl out to exchange it.

As soon as the magician had the lamp he gave

it a rub, and the genie appeared. 'Take Aladdin's house and everything in it far away to Africa,' he ordered. He planned to live there with the princess, and enjoy Aladdin's wealth.

When Aladdin returned and saw that his house and the princess were no longer there, he knew at once that the magician had tricked him. The lamp was gone, but he remembered the magic ring and gave it a rub.

'I am the slave of the ring,' said the genie. 'What is your wish?'

'Take me to the princess,' said Aladdin.

The genie carried him through the air to Africa, where the house now stood. Aladdin and Princess Badroulboudour embraced each other joyfully. Then Aladdin gave the princess a small phial and said, 'Tonight, when the magician is not looking, empty this poison into his wine.'

At the first opportunity that evening, the princess did as she had been asked.

*Aladdin and his princess… lived in happiness*

As soon as the magician drank from his glass, he fell back dead.

The lamp belonged to Aladdin once more, and he made a final wish: 'Take us and our home back to where we were before.'

This the genie did, and Aladdin and his princess lived together in happiness for many long years.

*It was a band of armed horsemen*

Ali Baba and Cassim were brothers who
lived in a town in Persia. Cassim was married to
a rich widow. He had a large shop and owned a
warehouse full of goods. Ali Baba was married to
a woman as poor as himself. He managed to earn
just enough to feed his family by cutting wood
and selling it in the town.

One day when Ali Baba was in the forest, he
saw in the distance a great cloud of dust. As he
watched, he realised that it was a band of armed
horsemen riding towards him. Fearing that they
might be thieves, he hid in a tree.

When the horsemen came near the tree
where Ali Baba was hiding, they dismounted and
tethered their horses. Then they lifted off their
saddlebags, which looked very heavy, and
followed their captain to a nearby rock.

'Open, Sesame,' said the captain.

A door, which Ali Baba had not noticed before, opened in the rock, and the brutish-looking men entered one by one. There were forty of them in all.

Ali Baba waited, and after some time he saw the men filing out again, now with empty saddlebags. When they were all out  Ali Baba heard the captain say, 'Shut, Sesame,' and the door in the rock closed. Each man fastened his saddlebag and mounted his horse, and they returned the way they had come.

As soon as the horsemen were out of sight, Ali Baba got down from the tree and went up to the rock. He was curious to see whether he could make the door open by using the same words that the captain had spoken.

'Open, Sesame,' he said boldly.

The door flew open, and Ali Baba saw an enormous cave filled with fantastic treasures piled high on top of each other. There were bales of silk, rolls of fine carpets, boxes of jewels and sacks full of gold coins.

Ali Baba knew that if the thieves came back they would surely kill him. So he wasted no time in wondering what to do. Quickly, he stepped inside the cave and pulled three sacks of coins up to the door. These he loaded onto his donkeys, covering them with sticks so that no one could see what they were. Then he said, 'Shut, Sesame,' to close the door again, and he set off for home.

Ali Baba's wife was so overcome at the sight of so much money that Ali Baba had to make her promise not to tell a soul about the treasure.

'Let me count them,' she begged, grabbing the coins and letting them run through her fingers.

'It will take too long,' said Ali Baba. 'Go and borrow a measuring cup from my brother Cassim while I dig a hole to bury the coins.'

Cassim's wife was curious about why her

sister-in-law wanted the cup. Ali Baba was so poor that they never had enough grain to measure. She dropped a little candle wax into the bottom of the cup where it would not be seen.

Ali Baba's wife went home and measured out the coins, filling the cup again and again. She was delighted to see how much money there was. Then, anxious to return the measuring cup as quickly as possible, she hurried back to her sister-in-law's house – never noticing that a piece of gold was sticking to the wax at the bottom.

Of course, Ali Baba's secret was discovered. When Cassim came home his wife said to him, 'You think you are rich, but I can assure you that Ali Baba is much richer than you are. He is so rich that he doesn't count his money – he measures it!'

Early the next morning Cassim went to visit Ali Baba, and showed his brother the piece of gold from the bottom of the cup.

*Ali Baba's secret was discovered*

'You pretend to be poor,' Cassim said, 'and yet you are measuring gold! How many of these gold pieces do you have? And where did you get them? Tell me the truth now, or I will hand you over to the sultan's guards!'

So Ali Baba told Cassim where he had found the coins. He even told him the exact words to use for opening the door in the rock. After all, he did not need to be greedy when there was plenty of treasure for them both.

The next day, Cassim set off with ten mules carrying large chests which he planned to fill with gold and jewels. He soon came to the place that Ali Baba had told him about, and found the door hidden in the rock.

'Open, Sesame!' he shouted. The door opened, and when Cassim was inside, it shut again.

Cassim was astonished to find even greater riches than he had imagined. He piled up as many bags of gold and other valuable items as he could carry. But when he wanted to open the door to get out, he could not remember the right words.

'Open, Barley,' he said uncertainly. The door stayed shut. 'Open, Wheat! Open, Corn!' Cassim tried over and over again, but it was no use. The door remained firmly closed.

At noon the thieves came to put more sacks in the cave. When they saw Cassim's mules, they said to one another, 'Someone must have found out how to get in. Don't let him get away!'

When the door opened, Cassim tried to rush out past the thieves. But they attacked him with their swords until they thought he was dead.

That night Cassim's wife was very worried. She went to Ali Baba and told him that her husband had not come back. So Ali Baba returned to the cave. There he found Cassim, badly wounded and left for dead by the thieves.

*She led him blindfolded to the house*

Ali Baba lifted his brother onto his donkey and brought him back home.

Ali Baba was met by Morgiana, Cassim's loyal housemaid.

'Your master is hurt and needs help,' he told her. 'But we must keep it secret, or we will all be in great danger.'

'I know someone who can help,' Morgiana said. 'He is an old shoemaker who is greatly skilled in healing, and he has saved many lives.'

Morgiana went to get the old man, and she led him blindfolded to the house. He bandaged Cassim's wounds and did everything he could for him. Then Morgiana led him back to his shop.

'Thank you for all you have done,' she said. 'And please, tell no one where you have been.'

Two days later, Cassim died.

After the funeral, Ali Baba and his family moved into the widow's house. Ali Baba's son went to work in Cassim's shop.

Some time later the thieves returned to the cave with more stolen treasures to add to their hoard.

Again their captain cried, 'Open, Sesame!' and again the door of the cave slid open. The thieves were amazed to find that Cassim's body had been taken away.

'Whoever rescued that man knows our secret!' said the bloodthirsty captain. 'We must find him and kill him!' The evil band agreed with their captain.

One of them offered to go into the town and act as a spy. Before long he came to the shoemaker's shop. By asking some clever questions, the thief was able to find out that the old shoemaker had recently tended to a badly wounded man.

'Take me to the house where this man lives, and I will give you a bag of gold,' said the thief.

'But I don't know where the house is,' the old man explained. 'I was blindfolded when I went there.'

'Then see if you can find it with your eyes closed,' said the thief.

With some difficulty, the shoemaker managed to lead the way to Cassim's house. The thief wanted to make sure that he did not miss the house when he returned with his companions, so he put a white chalk mark on the door.

A little later, Morgiana came out and saw the chalk mark. 'I wonder what this means,' she thought. 'Why is it only on our house, and not on the others?' Fearing that somebody was up to no good, she made chalk marks on several of the neighbours' doors. Then she went off to do her shopping.

When the thief came back, accompanied by

his companions, he found so many houses with white chalk marks that he could not tell which was the right one. The captain was very angry, and killed the thief at once. Although the other thieves were terrified, one of them volunteered reluctantly to play the spy. He, too, sought out the shoemaker and offered him money.

Next day the old shoemaker went with the second thief to find the house. When they got there, the thief put a red mark on the door.

Once again, Morgiana saw the mark and put similar marks on the neighbours' doors. The second thief was slain as quickly as the first.

This time the captain did not entrust the job to one of his men. He decided to go and find the house himself. The old shoemaker took him there as he had the others. But instead of making a mark on the door, the captain took a long, hard look at the house so that he would be sure to remember it.

The captain went back to his band of thieves. 'I want you to go and buy nineteen mules and thirty-eight large leather jars,' he said to them. 'One of the jars should be full of oil, and all the others should be empty.'

After they had followed the captain's orders, each thief got into an empty jar. All the jars, including the jar of oil, were loaded onto the gang's mules. The captain then led the mules to Ali Baba's house.

That evening Ali Baba was sitting at the open door of his home. When the captain told him that he was travelling to market with oil to sell, Ali Baba invited him to stay the night. He told the captain to leave the jars in the garden.

As he set each jar down, the captain managed to whisper to the thief inside, 'When you hear me throw a few stones from the window, come and join me.'

While Ali Baba was entertaining the captain,

Morgiana's lamp went out. There was no oil in the house, so she decided to take some from one of the jars in the garden.

As she approached the first jar, a voice whispered, 'Is it time?'

Morgiana was startled, but she quickly realised what was going on and calmed herself. 'Not yet, but soon,' she replied. She had to try several more jars before she found the one with oil in it, and she gave each thief the same answer.

Instead of lighting her lamp, Morgiana poured the oil into a kettle and put it on the fire. As soon as the oil was boiling, she tipped some into each jar. And that was the end of the thieves!

During the night, when everyone was asleep, the captain got up. Opening the window, he threw several stones at the jars. To his surprise, no one responded. He threw some more stones, and still more, until he began to grow very

*She approached the first jar*

uneasy. At last the captain went downstairs. When he smelled the hot oil, he realised immediately what must have happened. Finding that all the thieves were dead, he quickly made his escape.

In the morning Morgiana told Ali Baba everything that had happened. He was very grateful to her for her quick thinking, and promised he would never forget what she had done.

Meanwhile, the captain planned his revenge. Calling himself Cogia Houssain, he bought a shop close to the one where Ali Baba's son now worked. Before long he had made friends with the young man.

One day Ali Baba invited his son's new friend to dine with him. He did not realise that Cogia Houssain was the captain of the thieves, but Morgiana recognised him at once. 'He has come again to harm my master,' she thought.

Morgiana went to her room and put on a dancer's dress. Around her waist she fastened a belt, from which she hung a jewelled dagger. Then she covered her face with a veil.

'Bring your tabor,' she said to Abdallah, the manservant, 'and we will entertain the master's guest with music and dancing.'

Morgiana danced gracefully round the room to Abdallah's music. As she passed the captain, she plunged her dagger deep in his heart.

Ali Baba and his son watched in horror as Cogia Houssain fell down dead.

'What have you done? That man was our guest and a friend!' cried Ali Baba, angrily jumping to his feet.

*Morgiana and Ali Baba's son were married*

Morgiana opened the captain's cloak and showed Ali Baba a knife hidden there.

'If I had not killed him,' she said, 'he would have killed you instead. This man is not a merchant called Cogia Houssain. He is the captain of the thieves who came here concealed within the jars of oil!'

When Ali Baba realised that Morgiana was right, he embraced her. He asked her if she would like to marry his son and join his family.

So Morgiana and Ali Baba's son were married. In due course, Ali Baba taught his son the secret of the cave, which he in turn handed down to his son. With the riches they found there, they were all able to live in splendour for ever afterwards.